P9-BZE-954

The Frog Prince

Told by Diane Namm
Illustrated by Maurizio Quarello

One fine day a young princess walked down to the river. She took her favorite childhood toy with her, a shiny golden ball. She tossed it as high in the air as she could.

Before the princess could catch the ball, it bounced into the deep river nearby. The ball sank down, down, down to the very bottom. The princess wept bitterly at the loss.

"If I could get my ball back again, I would give all my jewels and everything I have," she said.

Just then, a frog popped his head out of the water.

"Princess, why do you cry?"
the frog asked.

"Silly frog. You can't help," the princess
replied. "My favorite ball fell into the
river, and I will never get it back."

"I don't want your jewels or anything you have. But I would like to see inside the palace," he said. "Let me visit you, and I will get your ball back."

Nonsense! the princess thought. *Frogs don't belong in palaces.*

But to the frog she said, "Of course, dear frog. If you get my ball, you may visit me whenever you like."

At once, the frog dived down to the bottom of the river. Moments later, he popped his head out of the water. The golden ball was in his mouth.

The princess plucked the ball from the frog's mouth. Without even so much as a thank-you, she ran back to the palace.

"Princess, take me too!" the frog called out to her.

The princess did not.

Next evening at dinner, she heard a *splish, splash, splish* upon the marble steps outside the palace door. Then she heard a gentle knock and a voice call out . . .

"Open the door, Princess dear.

Your one true love is here.

You must keep the promises you made

by the river deep in the greenwood shade."

The princess ran to open the door. There she saw the frog.

She was so frightened, she shut the door as fast as she could and ran back to her seat.

"What's wrong, dear Daughter?" asked the king.

"A silly frog retrieved my ball from the river. I promised he could visit me, and now he is at the door!" she replied.

"Promises must be kept, Daughter,"
the king advised. "Let the creature in."

Unhappily, the princess did as
she was told.

Splish, splash, splish.

The frog hopped onto the table.

"Princess, put your plate closer to me, so I may eat from it," said the frog.

The princess did. The frog ate till he could eat no more.

"Now I wish to sleep upon your pillow," yawned the frog.

The princess showed him to her room. The frog slept soundly.

In the morning he went *splish, splash, splish* down the stairs and out the door.

"Gone at last," sighed the princess.

But the frog returned the next night and sang the same love song. Again the princess allowed him to come in, eat from her plate, and sleep on her pillow.

And again the next morning he went *splish, splash, splish* out the door.

Then the frog returned for a third night! Again the princess allowed him to come in. But when the princess woke up the next morning, she saw a handsome prince with the most beautiful eyes standing at the foot of her bed.

"Who are you?" the surprised princess asked the young prince.

"I was the frog," he explained. "A cruel witch put a spell on me, but you have broken it by keeping your promise these past three nights."

The princess saw the goodness in the prince's beautiful eyes. The two fell in love instantly. They were married that day and drove off in an eight-horse carriage with plumes of feathers and wheels of gold. And they lived happily ever after.

STERLING CHILDREN'S BOOKS
New York

An Imprint of Sterling Publishing
387 Park Avenue South
New York, NY 10016

ISBN 978-1-4027-8429-3

Distributed in Canada by Sterling Publishing
c/o Canadian Manda Group, 165 Dufferin Street
Toronto, Ontario, Canada M6K 3H6
Distributed in the United Kingdom by GMC Distribution Services
Castle Place, 166 High Street, Lewes, East Sussex, England BN7 1XU
Distributed in Australia by Capricorn Link (Australia) Pty. Ltd.
P.O. Box 704, Windsor, NSW 2756, Australia

For information about custom editions, special sales, and premium and corporate
purchases, please contact Sterling Special Sales at 800-805-5489
or specialsales@sterlingpublishing.com.

Printed in China
Lot #:
2   4   6   8   10   9   7   5   3   1
07/13

www.sterlingpublishing.com/kids